# Disney
# MICKEY
# & FRIENDS

# Show-and-Tell
# Scout

By Calliope Glass

Illustrated by the Disney Storybook Art Team

NON-2015-0078 MYLAN IS A REGISTERED TRADEMARK OF MYLAN INC. THE QUESTIONS AND ANSWERS AT THE BACK OF THE BOOK ARE © 2015 MYLAN INC. ALL RIGHTS RESERVED.
NOT FOR RESALE.
COPYRIGHT © 2015 DISNEY ENTERPRISES, INC.
ISBN 978-1-4847-4489-5
FAC-029261-15307
PRINTED IN USA

*Disclaimer: The content of this book is not intended as medical advice. Families should check with their healthcare professionals regarding the treatment of severe food allergies.*

Content was developed by Disney and reviewed in consultation with Mylan Inc.

"Tag! You're it!" Scout said. He tapped Goofy on the shoulder and took off running.

"Gawrsh!" Goofy said.

Scout loved it when Mickey, Goofy, and the gang came over to play. They always had the best time!

"Scout, it's time to go to the doctor," Mrs. Fox called, poking her head out the back door.

"Aw, phooey," Scout said. "Can't we just play a *little* longer?"

Mrs. Fox shook her head. "You have to get your checkup before school starts."

"I love checkups!" Goofy said. "The doctor always gives me a lollipop!"

Scout pouted. He'd much rather keep playing with his friends, but he knew his mom was right. Waving sadly, he followed his mom to the car.

At the doctor's office, Dr. Li listened to Scout's heart. She shone a light in Scout's eyes. She peeked into his throat and asked him to say "Ahhh."

"Ahhh," Scout said.

"How are you doing with your food allergies, Scout?" Dr. Li asked. "Are you staying away from milk and peanuts?"

Scout nodded. He is severely allergic to milk and peanuts. If he ate even a little bit of either of them, he could get very sick.

Scout remembered the last time he had eaten something with milk in it by mistake. His stomach had started to hurt and he'd had trouble breathing. It had been very scary. Luckily, his parents knew that these were signs of a severe allergic reaction. They used his epinephrine auto-injector and took him to the hospital.

Scout was more careful now.

"We make sure to find out all the ingredients in something before Scout eats it," Mrs. Fox told Dr. Li. "And I always carry his auto-injectors with me in case there's an emergency."

"Are you excited about starting school?" Dr. Li asked.

Scout was excited, but Mrs. Fox looked nervous. "What if something happens when I'm not there to help?" she said.

Dr. Li suggested that Mrs. Fox make time on Scout's first day of school to talk to his teacher and the school nurse all about Scout's allergies and what to do in case he ate something he was allergic to. "I know it's hard to send Scout off without you, but he'll be okay. That's why you have an action plan," she said.

Dr. Li pointed to Scout's auto-injector. "I know you already have auto-injectors where you need them, but now that you're starting school, you'll need some to keep in the nurse's office, too," she said.

The doctor gave Mrs. Fox an extra prescription for school. Then she checked the expiration date on Scout's auto-injectors. "You should replace Scout's auto-injectors before they expire or if you have to use them."

"But hopefully we won't have to!" Scout said.

On the first day of school, Scout's mom took him to class. Mrs. Fox brought his school supplies, his lunch, and his severe allergy action plan. When it was Scout's turn to meet his teacher, Mr. Sanchez, Scout's mom was ready.

"Scout is severely allergic to peanuts and milk," Mrs. Fox explained.

"And broccoli!" Scout said.

"You are *not* allergic to broccoli," Scout's mom said. "And you still have to eat your veggies."

"Rats," Scout said. He gave his mom a sheepish grin. He knew his allergies were very serious, but he *really* didn't like broccoli!

Mrs. Fox told Mr. Sanchez all about Scout's allergies. She taught him which signs of an allergic reaction to look for and how to use Scout's auto-injectors. Mrs. Fox reminded Mr. Sanchez that if Scout ate something he was allergic to, they should call the nurse and seek emergency attention.

Finally, Mrs. Fox was sure that Mr. Sanchez understood how to take care of Scout. Giving Scout a kiss on the head, Mrs. Fox left to review Scout's action plan with the school nurse and give her his auto-injectors.

When all the parents were gone, Mr. Sanchez gave the kids cubbies and assigned seats. Scout could hardly believe his good luck. He was sitting at a table with his friends Connie, Andrew, and Emma.

Then Mr. Sanchez gave the kids their first homework assignment: to prepare a show-and-tell about themselves. Scout couldn't wait to get started.

Suddenly, Scout heard a familiar voice. It was Mickey!

"Mickey and Goofy are our classroom helpers this year," Mr. Sanchez explained. "They'll be helping you with your homework!"

Soon it was snack time.

"Oh, boy!" Scout said. His mom had packed him a great snack—a homemade muffin.

"I have pudding!" Connie said.

"I got pudding, too!" a boy named Matt said.

Listening to his friends, Scout felt a little left out. He couldn't eat pudding. It had milk in it.

"I have grapes!" Emma said.

"I have a sugar cookie!" a girl named Fatima said.

"Hey," Matt said, "let's trade snacks!"

Soon everyone at Scout's table was trading—pudding for cookies and cheese sticks for grapes.

Everyone except Scout, who held tight to the muffin his mom had made.

"I'll trade my pudding for your muffin," Matt told Scout.

Scout shook his head sadly. "No, thanks," he said. Scout could feel

himself blushing. He wished he could trade like everyone else, but it was too dangerous. What if he ate something with milk in it by accident? Or peanuts? He could get really, really sick.

"What's the matter?" Matt asked. He looked mad. "Don't you want to share? You think you have the best snack, and you want to keep it all for yourself?"

Just then, Mr. Sanchez looked over at Scout's table. "That's enough of that," he said. "Everyone, please eat the snack you brought."

Scout's friends groaned and grumbled, but everyone traded back. Scout breathed a sigh of relief.

"And, Matt," Mr. Sanchez said, "what's the rule?" He pointed at the sign on the classroom wall.

"No sharing food," Matt mumbled.

After school, Scout talked to Mickey and Goofy about his day.

"Today during snack time, everyone was trading snacks, but I couldn't join in," Scout said.

"Because of your alligators?" Goofy asked.

Scout laughed. "Yeah," he said, "because of my allergies. What if this is what school is like forever? What if I always feel left out?"

"How about you talk about your allergies for show-and-tell?" Mickey said. "Maybe it would be easier if people understood why you can't eat certain foods."

Scout thought that was a great idea!

The next day, Scout's class had show-and-tell. Soon it was Scout's turn!

"My name is Scout, and I'm allergic to peanuts and milk," he said. "I have to be really careful what I eat, and I can't share food, because if I have something I'm allergic to, I could get really sick."

Scout held up a picture he had drawn of his epinephrine auto-injectors. He explained what they were and how he used them.

Connie raised her hand. "What if you eat a peanut by accident?" she asked.

"Then I have to go to the nurse right away," Scout said. "My auto-injectors are in her office. They help to stop the allergic reaction from being so bad."

"How come I can eat peanuts and you can't?" Emma asked.

"I don't know," Scout said. He thought about it. "How come you have to wear glasses and I don't?"

Emma thought about it. "I guess everyone is different," she said.

"Yeah," Scout said. "Everyone is different!"

Scout was happy after show-and-tell. It felt good to know that everyone understood why he was so careful about food.

"Everyone did a great job today," Mr. Sanchez said when the presentations were over. "You all worked hard, and you were very brave to tell us about yourselves. So you all get a prize."

The teacher gave every single kid a pencil topper! Scout got a red troll, and Emma got a brown cat. Andrew got a green fish, and Connie got a red dragon.

Matt nudged Scout. "Hey," he said, "I'm sorry about yesterday. I didn't understand about your allergies."

"It's okay," Scout said. Then he noticed that Matt was looking at his red troll. It gave Scout an idea.

"I like your pencil topper," Scout said, pointing at Matt's blue bird. "Want to trade?"

"Yeah!" Matt said. The boys swapped pencil toppers. Scout loved his new blue bird!

"Emma, will you trade with me?" Connie asked. Soon all the kids were swapping pencil toppers.

Scout smiled. Maybe school would be fun after all!

# From Scout's World to Yours

### Sponsored by ▥Mylan

## What is a severe allergic reaction? What causes it?

Anaphylaxis is an allergic reaction that is rapid in onset and is life-threatening. Some people are more sensitive than others to triggers such as insect bites and stings, some medications, latex, and certain foods. The most common food-based causes of anaphylaxis in people with severe allergies are milk, eggs, peanuts, tree nuts, fish, shellfish, soy, and wheat. Anaphylaxis can also be caused by unknown triggers.

*Scout is allergic to milk and peanuts. What are you allergic to?*

## What are some of the symptoms of anaphylaxis?

Anaphylaxis can make someone feel sick in many different ways. You may feel dizzy or faint, have itchy skin or see a rash or hives, feel your lips or tongue swelling, have chest pain or trouble breathing, feel like your heart is beating very fast, vomit or have diarrhea, or something else entirely may happen. One of these symptoms by itself may not be a sign of anaphylaxis. If you are unsure if you have come into contact with one of your allergens, look for symptoms in two different systems of your body: for example, itchiness in your skin and a fast heart rate, or chest pain and hives.

*Scout knew he was experiencing anaphylaxis because his stomach hurt and he was having trouble breathing. What symptoms of anaphylaxis have you experienced?*

## What is an anaphylaxis action plan?

Anaphylaxis is unpredictable. Having a plan in place will help you and anyone taking care of you respond properly in case of a severe allergic reaction. An anaphylaxis action plan should list what you are allergic to and should include the signs and symptoms of anaphylaxis, the dose and location of your epinephrine auto-injectors (EAIs), and your emergency contact information.

You and your parents should work with your health care professional to develop this plan. Make sure to update your plan often, and share it with anyone who might take care of you, like a relative, a teacher, or your school nurse.

*Scout's mom shares his anaphylaxis action plan with his teacher and the school nurse. Who should you share your plan with?*

## Why does Scout carry two epinephrine auto injectors (EAIs)?

Epinephrine, also known as adrenaline, is a prescription medication that works to relieve the life-threatening symptoms of anaphylaxis. You should use your epinephrine auto-injector immediately if you are showing signs of a severe allergic reaction. Sometimes a single dose of epinephrine is not enough to slow down the symptoms of anaphylaxis, or the symptoms may go away and then come back. That's why it is important to carry two EAIs. Talk to your health care professional about how to use your EAI, and remember to always seek emergency medical care after using an EAI.

*Scout's mom keeps his auto-injectors in her purse and gives a set to the school nurse. Where do you keep your auto-injectors?*

**In the story, Dr. Li states that now that Scout is going back to school, he needs auto-injectors for the nurse's office. Why is this important?**

Those with severe allergies should have access to two epinephrine auto-injectors at all times. In the story, when Scout is not at school, he or his mom keeps his epinephrine auto-injectors nearby: for example, in Mrs. Fox's purse. When Scout is at school, his epinephrine auto-injectors are kept with the school nurse, who can give Scout the injection in the event of an emergency. **Remember, your EAI has an expiration date. Scout's mom always refills his prescriptions before they expire to make sure the epinephrine will work properly.**

*Where else do you think Scout should keep his epinephrine auto-injectors? Where do you keep yours?*

**Why can't Scout trade food with his classmates?**

Scout knows what foods he can't eat, but some foods may have "hidden" allergens in them that he isn't aware of. Eating something that he is allergic to could make him very sick. That's why it's important not to trade snacks with classmates. Your parents will send you to school with snacks they know are safe for you. The best way to prevent an allergic reaction is to always be aware of what you are eating and take steps to avoid anything that may contain items you are allergic to.

*Scout and his friends have fun trading pencil toppers instead of food. What can you trade with your friends in class instead of snacks?*

**Why is it good for Scout to tell his friends about his food allergies?**

Scout's mom tells his teacher and school nurse about his allergies and anaphylaxis action plan. It's good for Scout's friends to know about his allergies, too, so that they understand why he can't eat certain foods and so they can help him look out for his food allergies at school or during playdates.

*Scout tells his friends about his food allergies during show-and-tell. Have you told your friends about your food allergies?*